H. C Daniel

Love's Minstrel

And other Poems

H. C Daniel

Love's Minstrel
And other Poems

ISBN/EAN: 9783337206505

Printed in Europe, USA, Canada, Australia, Japan

Cover: Foto ©Andreas Hilbeck / pixelio.de

More available books at **www.hansebooks.com**

Love's Minstrel

AND OTHER POEMS.

BY

→ H. C. DANIEL. ←

London:

W. W. MORGAN & SON, HERNES HILL, PENTONVILLE, N.

1892.

BRADFORD:

PRINTED BY THORNTON AND PEARSON, THE COLLEGE PRESS,

BARKEREND ROAD.

Dedicated

TO

Charles E. Forshaw, LL.D.,

BRADFORD.

———◆•◆•◆———

LET but my muse in simple speech,
    The tone of admiration reach :
For one who with prolific pen,
Charms and instructs his fellow-men ;
Who, as a Poet, has a claim
To tread the foremost ranks of Fame—
Who, as a worker for his kind,
Breathes science with a deeper mind—
To him is this inscribed by me,
As pledge of Poet's sympathy.

H. C. DANIEL.

CAMBRIDGE,
    November, 1892.

PREFACE.

IN writing this short introductory Preface, I do not anticipate the judgment which the public may vouchsafe this work. The Author, who was for some time locally connected with this neighbourhood, is anxious that this connection should not pass unnoticed to the eyes of his many Yorkshire friends in issuing his first publication.

Mr. Daniel, who has received encouragement from such gentlemen as Professor Blackie and Mr. Walter Besant, should, to my mind, prove capable of carrying public opinion. Professor Blackie writes: "Your subjects are good, and your style is good. "Be faithful to your genius, and never write without "a strong inspiration." Mr. Walter Besant, M.A., the eminent novelist, also wrote him: "Your poems "have merit and show promise." I have therefore much pleasure in stating a hope that this small volume, though it may be somewhat stamped with immaturity, will, with due allowance, find proper appreciation.

WALTER J. KAYE, M.A.

ILKLEY COLLEGE, YORKSHIRE,
December 1st, 1892.

⭐ INTRODUCTION. ⭐

In minstrel garb, with light guitar,
He sang not to the tune of War,
Nor sang he ballads of the day,
Nor chanted high a border lay:
He courted not the glitt'ring throng,
Nor paid he homage to the strong;
He wander'd hence in changeful mood,
That spoke a course of restless blood,
And many wonder'd why he came
Without the minstrel's voice of fame:
Without the stirring speech of song
That honour'd Right and punished Wrong;
And lo, with his new minstrelsy,
A most uncommon Bard was he.

A simple tale, and duly told,
Without poetic shaping bold;
Though in its calm simplicity
It pleads a charm of purity:
That virtue of poetic strain
Spoke from the swelling heartstrings plain;
Like summer breezes, soft and clear,
It strikes with sweetness on the ear:
Dancing now with fervour bright
On its gay and wayward flight;
Pacing now with soften'd tread,
Gently murm'ring o'er the dead;
On and onward to the end
Does its spirit fast descend,
Gently asking, on its part,
If it cannot touch the heart.

❧ CANTO I. ❧

A LORDLY castle, tow'ring high
In all its awing majesty,
Frowns o'er a vale, a wood, a glade,
With calm and lovely spots to shade
The weary wand'rer, and inspire
His mind with one unmov'd desire:
To rest within the smiling peace,
Where warbling songsters e'er increase
Their melodies of piping notes,
Which, as they leave the swelling throats,
Are upwards as a tribute sent,
For blessings come and sorrows spent.

Without the wood, beneath a tree,
Stretch'd out in fashion lazily,
A youth in thoughtful mood is seen,
Half-hidden in his bed of green.

What is it in the form of face,
And in the charm of easy grace,
Which, to a stranger's seeking eyes,
Claim their attention and surprise?
Something, I trow, of import great,
To leave behind such telling weight.

The beauty of the spot is grand,
Consider'd from the eye's command!
A giant rock, with verdure dress'd,
Stands sentinel towards the west;
A living fountain, fresh and cool,
Trickling, trickling into a pool.
And to the south and east the fields,
Rich in the fulness of their yields,
Are mellow'd in the sunlight warm,
And given there and then a charm;
And far and near the cattle graze,
Calm and content beneath the rays:
While stately red and fallow deer,
Like phantoms, come to disappear;
And to the north, against the skies,
The castle towers darkly rise:
Firm on a rocky pinnacle
They make a worthy spectacle.

No wonder that the youth's delight
Is wholly centred on this site:
So pleasing to the mind and eye
In all its bright immunity.

With sudden move, he makes a stir,
Lo, in his hands, what has he there?
Yet hark! upon the air around
Is heard an unexpected sound:

Softly across the verdant plains
Sweep plaintively the measur'd strains,
Until fair Nature, far and near,
Nurs'd in a blossom'd atmosphere,
Seems to respond in voicèd play,
As echoes come and die away.

Still with a magic touch so rare
He sends the music through the air,
And then his voice, with gentle pow'r,
Swells forth in rapture of the hour.

"The noonday sun beams overhead,
    The zephyr lightly sighs ;
Above is heard the merry bird
    Full of its melodies.

The woodbine casts its luscious scent
    Around the forest glade ;
While myriad flow'rs in rustic bow'rs,
    Bedeck its gloomy shade.

The rugged scars of deep ravines
    Show many a wretched path
Where cascades vent in cragg'd descent
    Their loud unbroken wrath.

The sun-tipp'd hills in splendour shine
    Against the purple sky,
And thoughts in song are borne along
    From low-born lips and high."

The voice, about to sing again,
Continues not the sweet refrain :
He, with a movement quick and shy,
Lets fall his charmer hastily ;

His eyes, which in amazement look,
Have but their pow'r of will forsook :
Their fasten'd gaze, to strain'd extent,
Are on a lovely maiden bent,
Whose gentle form and kindly face
Give an enchantment to the place.

" Sir Minstrel," quoth the lovely maid,
As she a studied curtsey made,
" Look not astonish'd that you see
A stranger in your sanctuary.
I would not trespass, but your skill
Quite overpower'd my better will ;
And with the frailty of my kind,
I vow'd I would Sir Minstrel find."

Still fix'd the youth his startled gaze,
Unmov'd by his admirer's praise ;
Nor yet in speech can he reply,
So quick this strange discovery.
She nearer comes, and bends her down,
And sweeps him with her snow-white gown,
As taking up the light guitar,
She strikes the chord with fingers fair,
And in a voice so rich and sweet,
That makes his heart the faster beat,
She sings a love-song then and there
Of damsel's scorn and knight's despair :—

　　" Wilt thou be mine, oh maiden,
　　　　And take a knightly name ?
　　I come with honours laden,
　　　　With riches and with fame ;
　　My castle waits with open gates
　　　　To give my love a home :
　　A palfry white shall bear thee light,
　　　　So come, my fair one, come."

"Thy love I could not foster,"
  The maiden fast replied ;
"Thou art a deep imposter,
  Whose tongue has surely lied.
Thy name it bleeds with dark misdeeds,
  Which would but honour stain ;
So, knight, depart with thy false heart ;
  Go single home again."

The knight in wrath retreated,
  For truth is ever strong ;
For once he was defeated
  In painting right with wrong ;
He spurr'd his horse in dark remorse
  Upon his lonely way :
Sought love again, but still in vain,
  For many weary day."

With heighten'd blush the songstress turns
And notes the self-same fire burns
Upon the visage of the Bard,
Whose eyes are fixed upon the sward.

"Come, come, Sir Bashful, is it thus
A student's merits you discuss ?
Or have I, in my self-taught way,
But rendered half my chosen lay ?
Look up, look up, no ogress here
Sits hunger'd on your throne of fear."

Still with a mute's despairing sense,
He proves too weak in confidence ;
Though not too weak for modest glance
Towards the speaker's countenance.

"Come, Innocence, I pray you find
The one great gift of human kind;
I truly understand and see
Your lack of merry company.
And yet methinks that handsome face
Has power a nobler dress to grace:
That voice, so delicate of tone,
Should far superior parents own;
In fact, your presence seems to me
Full of a charming mystery."

" Fair lady," quoth the minstrel youth,
" My looks are traitors to the truth;
My voice, though trained to meet the lyre,
Works not with intellectual fire:
But with compliance to thy will,
Let me unite it to my skill;
For by the Muse's pleasant test
Can I replace the voidness best."

And to a prelude, soft and sweet,
Is joined his voice in verses meet:—

"I sat one night on a lonely brae,
As the moon gave forth its tinsel ray,
And the elfin rangers sought their play
    Near flow'ry nooks,
    And murm'ring brooks,
I heard their mystic voices singing,
Tun'd to their harps in measure ringing,
As o'er the moonlit valleys winging,
    Tripping it, skipping it,
     Merrily they,
    Wantonly, hastily,
     Recklessly gay,

Theirs is the night to make,
Dawn must their revels break :
Free from the waking world,
Down in their caverns curl'd,
Wrapt from the sun must be,
Their own sweet mystery.

Now while I sat on that lonely brae
A form came down on a soft moon ray :
Her golden hair in the western wind
Danc'd as it swept to her waist behind ;
Her lovely face, like a symbol of love,
Was proof that she came from the realms above,
And 'neath her arms two delicate things,
A pair of beautiful angel's wings.

'Why sit ye alone 'neath the midnight sky
With a look so sad in your youthful eye ?
Why sit ye alone when souls of sin
Are all laid out in their cloaks within ?
Is it to seek for a mystic pow'r
That you brave the sprites of this solemn hour.

'I sought the night for its soothing spell,
To hear the elves in their fairy dell ;
And happy were I if I could be
Enroll'd in their charms of mystery.'

'Then come with me on my stream of light,
And view the aerial joys of night :
The breeze shall tune my voice on high,
To sing an elfin tragedy.'

Her magic wand a circle made,
Her voice its influence convey'd ;
My earthly essence lost its weight

Beneath the charm of mystic state;
And this in a tone so sweet and soft,
Is what I heard in my ride aloft :—

' I once belong'd to the elfin throng,
    And tripp'd the velvet sward ;
My sire, beloved by his vassals true,
    Was a great elfin lord.

And every night in the kingly train,
    His stately form would be :
And every night to the music light,
    His step was quick and free.

He danc'd with the queen in emerald robe,
    Within the royal ring :
My mother receiv'd the honour too
    Of dancing with the king.

One night the king, in a merry voice,
    Bade send a slave for me ;
The slaves of the elfin world I trow,
    Work not in slavery.

And when I came at the king's command,
    He bent on me his glance,
And placing his arm around my waist,
    We tripp'd the merry dance.

' You step it well,' said the elfin king,
    And press'd his lips to mine ;
The bride of our darling prince shall be,
    With such fair grace as thine.'

He call'd his courtiers all around,
    And told them of his choice ;
The news of the bridal of their prince
    Made ev'ry soul rejoice.

But a wicked fairy chanc'd to hear
  The news of this our troth,
And as she wish'd for the prince's hand,
  Her heart was very wroth.

She sent me a prancing palfry white
  All the way from Snowdon:
It was the best and the fleetest steed
  That elf maid e'er rode on.

The night for our wedding nuptials came:
  The prince, the king, and queen,
Were with their brilliant court encamp'd
  Upon the merry green.

And I was dress'd in a vi'let robe,
  A lily in my hair;
And all proclaim'd and honour'd me,
  The fairest of the fair.

So off we went, such a happy band,
  And I was gay indeed:
Riding along to the courtly throng
  Upon my milk-white steed.

But curs'd be that wicked fairy's name,
  That she our hopes should blight;
For up thro' the air that Snowdon mare
  Carried me out of sight.

Up thro' the midnight air went we
  For thirty nights or more,
Until with a quick and sudden dash
  We reach'd the moon's bright shore.

And out from a cave an aged man
  Came forth with step and slow:
'What seekest thou from the Queen of Night,
  From elfin realms below?'

Then spoke the steed, with a magic voice,
    ' I bring to thee a maid
As a present from the fairy sprite
    Who keeps the silent glade.

Give her the wings for the night to roam,
    Thy lady's charms to spread ;
Give her the light of thy moonbeams bright,
    And crown it round her head.'

Away to the earth sped back the steed,
    And left me there alone ;
While the old man mumbled to himself,
    And in his cave was gone.

But as I sat on that lonely shore
    A spirit came to me,
And brought me the wings and magic wand
    Which carries you so free.

And this is the tale of maiden's grief,
    Of her who sings to-night ;
Yet ever gay, with her beaming ray,
    For him, her princely wight."

The last line trembling in his throat,
Dies faintly on the ending note,
And timidly a look is cast
Upon the maid in rapture fast.

She smiles approvingly and cries,
With finger rais'd and beaming eyes :
' Oh ! minstrel if you cannot teach,
At least the heart you surely reach ;

And for the choice of speech, I own
I much prefer the measur'd tone.
Take this, oh most enchanting Bard,
And keep it as fair maid's reward,
With hopes that future days will see
Our voices tuned in unity.

In manner courteous and grand,
She takes the minstrel's willing hand;
Whereon, to friendship's golden plight,
Is plac'd a ring of lustrous light.
Then once again, with charming smile,
She sings in fascinating style;
Her eyes fix'd on the landscape fair,
The zephyr mingling with her hair.

" The merle is heard with the mavis here,
   The cuckoo calls its mate;
The roebuck bounds with a sense of fear,
   While hunters ride in state:
      With arrows true
      And bows of yew,
   To course it down to fate.

Their horns burst forth with a startling sound,
   And hark! they come this way;
Along o'er the merry green they bound,
   To sweep upon their prey:
      Lo, to the chase,
      At reckless pace,
   They come, they come this way."

And on the still and balmy air,
The hunting horns create a stir;

And fast the huntsmen down the wood
Come galloping in merry mood.
With buckskin hose and jerkin green,
A merrier lot ne'er was seen ;
And lo, in fright the maid is gone,
While he, alas, is left alone.

CANTO II.

Once more the foliage of that tree
Sheds over them its canopy:
For Time works out a magic thread,
Unbroken only by the dead.
Once more the instrument unstrung
Is ready for the song unsung:
The voice, whose tuneful accents bring
A crowd of mem'ries on the wing;
Let them be blessed if they will,
The Muse makes them more blessed still;
Let them be sorrow's harsh alloy,
It gives the pain a soothing joy:
Dark is our worldly liberty,
But how much darker without thee.

So think the twain, as face to face,
They breathe the glory of that place;
Unchalleng'd by the cry of Care,
The present bright, the future fair.

'Sweet Constance, can I e'er repay,
In aught but small, unworthy way,
The love which with our joys imparts
A sacred spell upon our hearts ?
Have I, a minstrel, any power
To bless thee with a rich endower ?
Which by thy lordly sire's name,
Must be the life blood of the claim."

In answer to this meek appeal,
A rosy flush is seen to steal
Across the maiden's visage fair,
From dimpled cheek to chestnut hair,
And with an artful look and sly,
That spoke an unbelieving eye ;
She strikes with gentleness the strings
And softly to her lover sings :—

    "Tell me that the moon is yonder,
      Where that kingly orb is bright,
    Rather than in dreamland ponder
      On the way to darken light.

    Tell me that the stars no longer
      Gleam athwart the ev'ning sky,
    Rather than thy will be stronger
      In the use of falsity.

    Tell me that the heart can never
      Beat without love's purity,
    Rather than a guise should sever,
      Cupid's bond of unity."

His eyes reflect a sudden light
As daylight sweeps away the night,
And 'neath the outward form is seen,
An untold force of working keen.

" The time has come when hearts should know
The sources whence their love springs flow ;
The time has come when truth should clear,
The clouds which dull love's atmosphere ;
To greet with undisguised ray
The dawning of a brighter day."

He takes a note from out his breast
With a silken chord and seal press'd ;
And, with a studied move and bland,
He gives it in the maiden's hand.

" Take this, sweet maid, but look not in
Until the ev'ning mists begin ;
Read it within thy maiden bow'r,
In silence of the midnight hour ;
And when the morrow's sun is high,
I'll come to hear those lips reply."

Then in a fitful mood again
His voice is measur'd to a strain.

" Like a merry bird I wander'd here,
With a voice of song for Cupid's ear ;
With a heart full gay
Where the sun beams play,
And the woodland flow'rs are peeping ;
Like a merry bird my song is high,
Impell'd by the heart's great ecstasy,
On the wind's sweet breath.
O'er the summer heath,
Where the insect's hum is sweeping.

Like a murm'ring stream my course I take,
Through the open glen and ferny brake ;
With a whisper sweet,
For the things I meet,
To my reckless tune of roving :

Like a murm'ring stream my course is long,
Free from the noise of the busy throng,
    And thus have I come
    From my distant home
To conquer a heart worth loving."

Then comes a change, their youthful eyes
Are fill'd with questions and replies;
Their hands entwine, the birds above,
Sing to the concord of their love;
The butterflies around them rest,
And for a vantage ground contest;
The lazy drone, in flitting by,
Forgets its winter's misery;
The busy bee from clover sweet
Gathers and stores by mouth and feet,
And now and then upon the air,
The neighbouring kine create a stir;
While thro' the ferny foliage near,
The timid roebuck comes to peer,
Embolden'd by the gentle strains
Which float around its green domains;
And over all, supreme in one,
In regal splendour is the sun.

Anon, the damsel, flush'd and gay,
Commences on the chords to play;
And then as if the will commands,
The voice joins with the active hands.

   "Oh! let me live, where beauty smiles
     Adorn'd with Nature's treasures;
  Where Fancy's realm of borrow'd wiles
     Succumbs to living pleasures;
  Where hearts and minds can truly find
     A power of adoration,
  And passions leave no trace behind
     Of sinful concentration.

Where souls are tun'd by Nature's voice
    For realms of greater beauty,
And life seems always to rejoice
    In action of its duty ;
Where happiness and glory shine,
    And wonders never ceasing ;
Where heav'nly things with earth combine,
    The peace of man increasing."

His face in admiration strong,
Tells that the heart approves the song ;
While she with loving eyes aglow,
Speaks sweetly to the Bard and low.
"What was it that you wish'd to say,
Ere we had parted yesterday ?
News of importance I should guess,
And therefore beg you to confess."
" Nay, thou art wrong, my pretty bird,
Important should be term'd absurd ;
For things by what they first appear,
May after all be far from clear.

So let my words pass as they seem,
The outcome of a nightly dream,
And as our love, our hours of bliss,
Have been in unity with this,
Our speech, fair one, should sometimes be
Exchang'd upon its melody.

    " I saw a figure in my sleep,
        Cloth'd in sable mourning ;
    Which in a voice sepulchr'lly deep,
        Gave to me a warning.

    And this is what it surely said ;
        " Rouse thee up, awaken !
    For danger sits upon thy head
        Love must be forsaken ?

It lifted up a gory hand,
    And, with movement lastly,
Tore from it's cover'd breast a band,
    Showing a wound ghastly.

When I awoke the figure still
    Seem'd to be before me :
Yet from this moment come what will
    I shall e'er adore thee."

The sun, in setting to the west,
Is peeping o'er the rocky crest ;
The day has worn, the hour has come
For them to take their pathway home.

So tender are the words they speak,
    As yonder glows the sunset red ;
That blushes ripen on each cheek
    As closer brings each one their head.
Then comes the sound of lips that meet
    And seal the burning kiss divine ;
Their hearts with loving candour beat,
    Their eyes with heav'nly pow'r shine.
She asks him, softly, " sing once more,
    Before I part from you to-day ;
His fingers answer with the score,
    His voice throws out the parting lay :—

" Oh ! when alone how slow time seems
    Its measured force to trace,
Yet when o'er me thy presence beams,
    How quick its fleeting pace.

The feather'd songster's always free
    To woo its chosen mate ;
Yet now I have to part from thee,
    And leave our hopes to fate.

When gone, thy being lives again
   In fancy near my heart ;
And though to separate gives pain,
   Our souls are ne'er apart.

The thought of this creates new life,
   And keeps my spirit gay ;
It proves the victor in my strife,
   And cheers my lonely way."

Gone is the being, lost to view,
   Adown the shady vista green,
And dearly does the hero rue
   The absence of his angel queen.
He sits in melancholly mood,
   And ponders long in silence drear,
While twilight gathers round the wood,
   And life seems resting far and near.
At last with ev'ning's soft advance
   Along the deep'ning sky above,
He casts away the joyless trance,
   And from the place is seen to move.

But as the lover homeward bound,
   Builds high his castles in the air ;
He fails to hear another sound,
   Which bids him there and then beware.
On ! On ! he goes ; yet not alone,
   For look ! a form is seen to spring ;
The youthful Bard, without a groan,
   Sinks to the earth, a lifeless thing.

➤✳ CANTO III. ✳◀

WHEN sprites their nightly visits make,
 And shadows haunt the sighing wind;
When owls their secret nests forsake
 To cast their hootings o'er mankind;
When mystic noises fill the air,
 And restless brains with dreams contest;
When worldly happiness and care
 Are in the pow'r of sleep and rest:

Do not these mysteries of night
 Create an awe-inspiring spell;
Which, though destroy'd by morning light,
 Is soon restor'd at vesper bell.

To-night the moon in brilliant ray,
 Shines o'er the fertile plains around;
The stars their homage to her pay,
 For they with glitt'ring light abound.

The gentle wind from southern seas,
  Is full of whispers soft and low ;
Its sweet caress upon the trees
  Creates a trembling to and fro.
On, on it wanders, calm and free,
  It comes! 'tis gone! yet comes again ;
While in our own obscurity,
  We seek to find its end in vain.

It passes onward to a wood
  Near which a stately castle towers ;
It lingers where those lovers stood
  Amidst the sweetly scented bowers.
On, on, it goes in dancing glee,
  Yet hark! it gives a sudden swell ;
It makes a strange discovery,
  In shape an awful spectacle.

A human form, so young, so fair,
  Is by this southern wand'rer found ;
The livid face, the ghastly stare,
  Is answered by the crimson ground.

And near the murder'd minstrel lies
  His lov'd and treasured instrument ;
Which by the breeze with sudden cries,
  Is challeng'd light and reverent.

WIND.—

  Oh! charmer, who is it I see
    In this poor mangled lifeless heap ?

MUSE SPIRIT.—

  ' He was our prince of minstrelsy,
    Hence on thy way, oh! wind and weep.'

WIND SPIRIT.—

> 'Come let me hear his story true,
>   That I may sing it on my way;
> And for his soul my sweetest dew,
>   Shall greet in double form the day.'

MUSE SPIRIT.—

> Come, rest thee with thy ocean breath,
> And kiss the face so white in death,
>   While whis'pring low,
>   I tell thee how
> His tender heart was made a sheath.

> "There liv'd a youth, a goodly child,
>   With pure and gentle mind;
> A subject of Euterpe's will,
> He was an Orpheus in skill,
>   Thou knew him, Southern Wind.

> He used to wander near this wood,
>   And dream throughout the day;
> While frequent ditties tun'd by me,
> Would swell this sweet locality,
>   Through Love's inspiring sway.

> A lovely maiden, passing once,
>   By chance she heard his voice;
> Her heart in wonderland was caught,
> And for the subtle cause she sought,
>   Which made her heart rejoice.

> These two, from day to day, in love,
>   Were firmly bound by me;
> But yester night, with crafty tread,
> A mantled demon struck him dead,
>   From dark pent jealousy.

She sits within yon castle halls,
  Yet knows not of his fate ;
With thou, oh wind, thy night course steer,
And whisper comfort in her ear,
  Her lover's end relate.

Tell her to fetch me in the morn,
  In mem'ry of their love ;
And when the culprit's form is by,
My chords shall burst in liberty,
  'That I, his guilt may prove."

Again the wind pursues its course
  'Towards the castle on the hill ;
Its passage seems as if remorse
  Has checked its gay and buoyant will.
Around the walls, with moans and sighs,
  Its mystic voice is heard to glide ;
Until it suddenly descries
  The maiden's casement open'd wide,
And there upon her couch so white,
  She quietly breathes in peace and rest ;
The moon it sheds its silv'ry light
  Upon her soft and naked breast.

She starts anon in silent dread,
  The mystic voice attracts her ear ;
It seems to dance around her head,
  And then to quickly disappear.

Again it comes and whispers low,
  This time its voice is plainly heard ;
"Oh ! maiden let me share thy woe,
  For I too loved the handsome Bard."

"What voice is this that I can hear,
   Which asks to share a maiden's grief?
Has the Almighty heard my prayer,
   To give this aching heart relief."

"My voice is from the southern seas,
   Where Afric's brazen face is seen;
Thou callest me the choral breeze,
   That wets the lips of nature green.
Before when I have pass'd this way,
   Thy brow I've often stopp'd to kiss;
And I remember thou wouldst say,
   That thou to me ow'd half thy bliss."

"'Tis true, oh! southern wind, 'tis true,
   Yet now your fragrance does not cheer;
For with your mighty robe of dew,
   You bring to me a sense of fear.
I thought you spoke to me just now,
   And mentioned woe with minstrel youth;
And since of him you needs must know,
   I ask you to relate the truth."

WIND.—

   'Then maiden list and hear me,
     Full rife is dreaded hate;
   For though I come to cheer thee,
     I bring thy heart a weight.

   As I my course was steering
     Across this land to-night;
   I, in my gay careering,
     Receiv'd a sudden fright.

   Beneath a silver beech tree
     A mangled corpse I saw;
   The sight will ever teach me,
     To pass that spot in awe.

And near its murder'd master
A light guitar was found ;
And as I glided faster,
An impulse kept me bound.

I therefore ceas'd my sighing,
And stopp'd my gentle speed ;
And with my voice complying,
I ask'd about the deed.

Then spoke the lonely charmer,
In agony of tone ;
About the night's sad drama,
And how the deed was done.

It told me of thy meeting,
And of thy treasur'd plight :
Of heart's united beating ;
Of the jealous weapon bright.

It spoke a rival's anger,
And bade me tell thee this ;
That thou art still in danger
Of burning 'neath his kiss.

It said if thou would'st let it
Near to thy person be ;
Thy meeting with the culprit,
Its tighten'd chords would free.

So take this friendly warning,
Let not thy heart despair ;
Go fetch it in the morning,
And foster it with care.

And now I must be going :
Remember in thy mind,
When winter storms are blowing,
Thy friend, the southern wind."

The moon still sheds its welcome beams,
    The wind still whispers as before ;
And yet what tale is this that seems
    Confus'd with charms of magic lore ?
'Tis but the influence of sleep,
    With mystic realizations bound ;
Which o'er the resting damsel creeps,
    As she in deep repose is found.

❧ CANTO IV. ❧

ENTHRON'D within his humble cell,
A cavern in a rocky dell,
A hermit, past the prime of age,
Liv'd out his blunted pilgrimage.
His meagre face, with a beard dress'd,
Flow'd white and lengthy o'er his breast,
And tipp'd a girdle round his waist.
Which a tatter'd robe of sackcloth graced,
The scanty locks about the head,
Were numbered closely with the dead ;
While in the eyes a sacred fire
Burn'd with repeated fasting higher ;
Which drew respect with a fierce glare
From angry scorn and a driv'lling air ;
And calmly glow'd with peaceful heat,
In contact with behaviour meet.

His gloomy cell by nature wrought,
Was in its simple portion fraught,
Except a few thing scatter'd loose,
Awaiting but their time of use.
A truckle bed, with skins of deer,
A chisled nook half bare of cheer;
A stool, and sundry books of lore,
Scatter'd promiscuous the floor.
Nothing of luxury was seen,
That object of a hermit's spleen,
Except a fire of faggots bright,
For the dual use of warmth and light.

Without the cell, a wooded park;
Loom'd on its border drear and dark;
For night had come, and on its back
Storm clouds were riding thick and black.
The atmosphere around was close,
The birds had sought their night's repose;
And kine the open land forsook,
For some remote and shelter'd nook.

Emerging from the woodland side,
The hermit's form was seen to glide;
Full anxious in the one idea,
Of 'scaping from the downfall near.

His threshold was but hardly gain'd
Before the frghtful deluge rain'd;
Preceded by the light'ning flash
And heavy boom of thunder crash;
Which shook the very rocks below,
With all the force of madden'd foe.

The hermit in his barren cell,
  Drew nearer to the friendly fire ;
And as the storm was heard to swell,
  Built up the burning faggots higher.
All of a sudden a voice was heard,
  It call'd for help, if help was nigh ;
The old man strok'd his snow white beard,
  And left his shelter rapidly.
He soon return'd, and with him one
  Whose noble form, and handsome face,
Were doubly in themselves alone
  A passport for that hermit's grace.
His costly garb though soil'd and wet,
  Contrasted with the place around ;
And could no look of dire regret,
  Upon his countenance be found.
And there within the glowing light,
  On friendly conversation bent ;
They bade defiance to the night,
  And on the whole appear'd content.

HERMIT.—

    How came thee, friend, to wander forth
      On such a night, at such an hour ;
    Methinks a sign of heaven's wrath,
      Could hardly be the acting pow'r."

STRANGER.—

    "Why father ! truly thou art right,
      But fortune seem'd in different mood ;
    For e'er the storm commenc'd to-night,
      I was within St. Stephen's Wood.
    I did not see the sign of war,
      Embedded in my heavy shade ;
    And that is how I came too far,
      And in unconscious humour stray'd.'

HERMIT.—

> " Art thou a guest of yonder lord ?"

STRANGER.—

> "Ay, father, thou art right again,
>> Lord Stephen keeps a merry board,
> And I the gayest in the train."

HERMIT.—

> "Then thou art he whom folks declare,
>> To be the lady's chosen groom ;
> Little thought I her great despair,
>> Would e'er have left that forest tomb."

The hermit from his stock of fuel,
> Supplied the burning heap once more ;
Then sat him down upon his stool,
> With eyes fix'd on the lighted floor.

STRANGER.—

> " Come, father, thou art now sedate,
>> This storm has cast a gloomy spell ;
> Yet while the lull of it we wait,
>> A story I should like full well.
> In yonder castle, on a wall,
>> A light guitar allures the eye ;
> Its chords are broken one and all,
>> And shrivell'd in complexity.
> I know that once it did belong,
>> To one who lov'd my future bride ;
> Whose life of innocence and song,
>> Was void of greater will to guide.
> I know that by a rival's hand
>> He fell within that forest's shade ;
> That yonder, where three beeches stand,
>> His corpse was by her orders laid.

I know not how the vengeance came
  Upon the victim's crafty foe ;
Nor why the charmer's wond'rous fame
  Is e'er the talk of high and low.
Come, father, thou wilt surely tell
  The ending which I crave to hear ;
For thou must recollect it well;
  Living upon the spot so near."

The hermit's piercing eyes were bent
  Upon his young companion's face ;
But in a voice of calm consent,
  He answered with a comely grace.

" I know it well, yet in good sooth,
  My tale should be of God and heav'n ;
But draw thee closer in, Sir Youth,
  While I relate the judgment giv'n."

The Hermit's Story.—

St. Stephen's halls resounded gay,
With flowing bowl and merry lay ;
The song was high, the wine full red
Ascended to the weakling's head.
Many jested and many jok'd,
And some they laugh'd, while some, provok'd,
Cast down a gauntlet in their ire,
And flash'd the sword with fool's desire ;
Until in tow'ring voice their lord,
Renew'd the peace around his board.

Now many were the suitors came,
With handsome face and knightly name ;
To give their love and seek the hand
Of her, the mistress of the land.

They brought her presents from the East,
Right costly was the very least ;
From India's resplendent shore,
They brought her charms of magic lore ;
From Persia, jewels of sparkling light,
From Turkey, robes of spotless white,
While Italy and merry Spain,
Were far from visited in vain.

Now spake Lord Stephen out aloud,
And call'd attention from the crowd,
While forth a minstrel calmly stepp'd,
As o'er the chords his fingers swept,
And with his voice he claim'd to say,
The orders of his lord to-day.

    ' Wooers get ready
    Your hands unsteady
To play on the gifted string, O ;
    Voices relying
    On love's replying
Must come on the Muse's wing, O.

    Voices not singing,
    Love useless bringing,
And this is my lord's command ;
    Hearts must not falter
    'Neath Cupid's altar,
So come with your voice and your hand.'

Many a heart was stricken sad,
  Many a voice gave out a sigh ;
Only three with faces glad,
  Forward came their luck to try.

The youngest first a comely boy,
Struck on the chords with seeming joy.

' Watchful guards the night are keeping
  On the battlements afar ;
Higher still the clouds are sweeping,
  O'er the dreaded face of war.
Hark ! with sudden cries resounding,
  Comes the warning of surprise,
Steel from mail'd breast rebounding,
  Spark on spark with danger flies.

' On, for Britain's king and glory,'
  Is the cry which rends the air ;
' Let our weapons, stain'd and gory,
  Strike the rebels with despair.'
Then the cry of ' no surrender,'
  Breaks from those within the walls ;
' To the death each brave defender,'
  Seeks the battle till he falls.

As the morning sun is glowing
  On the castle bright and red ;
From its keep a standard flowing
  Royally dances o'er the dead.
Victors in their ghastly armour,
  Seeking now the sunlight sweet,
Ponder on the midnight drama,
  And their brothers in defeat.

Fair Constance turn'd with mark'd contempt,
At this the very first attempt.

" Is this the way you come to seek
The blushes from a damsel's cheek ?
With death and blood and battle wage ;
Methinks 'tis fitter for a page."

The second forward came and took
The instrument, with evil look
Towards the minstrel sitting there,
Beneath the maid's exalted chair.
He was a knight arm'd *cap-a-pié*
With all the blaze of chivalry,
The vizor lower'd to its place,
Cover'd from all the inside face ;
And well it was that it could be,
With such an evil look to see.
His hands uncover'd for the song,
Were full of muscles hard and strong.

He to the minstrel bending down,
Spoke low, and with a threat'ning frown.

KNIGHT.—

   'What art thou doing, devil, here ? '

MINSTREL.—

   'I yearned perforce for better cheer ? '

KNIGHT.—

   'Then if this day I weather not,
   Look to thine own endanger'd lot.'

He took his place, and bold and free,
Began his chosen melody.

   'LIST ! while to thee I play,
   Love's softest roundelay ;
   Brought from its palace sweet,
   Sung at thy treasur'd feet ;
   Hope's strings are ringing gay,
   List ! to my roundelay.'

What's that ? as o'er the chords again
His fingers mov'd, but mov'd in vain,
For with a sharp and sudden twang,
The broken strings with discord rang ;
And he, confus'd as to the cause
Of this strange, unrehearsed pause,
Held up the instrument on high,
And swept it with a direful eye.

What's that upon the surface show'd,
And to those eyes with brightness glow'd ?
A brightness that was full and red,
Which spoke of blood in anger shed ?
What's that upon his hand again,
Which look'd withal a crimson stain ?
A stain that he liked not to see,
So full of bloody mystery.

He cast the fearful thing away,
In tone of harsh and fierce dismay.

Forth stepp'd the startled maid, and quick,
And up the instrument did pick ;
And turning to her lordly sire,
With a pale face and eyes afire :
She pointed with a trembling hand,
And waited for his stern command.

Up started Stephen's stately form,
To burst the dreaded thunderstorm.

" What's this, base Knight, that thou hast done
    Within the darkness of our wood ?
What devil's bounty hast thou won,
    By shedding pure and noble blood ?

Thrice noble is the memory
  Of him, who 'neath St. Stephen's lies;
The youngest son of Lord Magee,
  Who wander'd hither in disguise.
The charge is made, and thou art free
  To clear this day thy tainted name;
But until then I make decree,
  And brand thee with a felon's shame."

And forth there came a gallant knight,
  Who in his branded comrade's face,
Cast the defiant gauntlet bright,
  And drew his weapon from its case.

Then rang their swords with angry peal,
And flash'd the sparks from meeting steel,
        As high or low
        They struck the blow
  To bring each other down.
" Come, stand thee to the devil's throne,
The deed, thou dark assassin, own,
        Or purge from blame
        Thy tainted name,
  And stand by honour's crown."

Full thick and hard the cuts were given,
And many a seam in corselet riven,
        As right and left
        With handling deft
  They both alternate press'd.
Dark flash'd the eye of branded knight
Beneath his vizor's narrow light,
        As thrice there came
        With deadly aim
  A blow upon his crest.

Slowly the strokes; their telling pow'r
Number'd the victim's final hour,
  With stagg'ring gait
  He falls, too late,
 Too late for mercy's plea.
"Come, stand thee close, my foeman brave,
My sword and spurs thou yet canst save,
  Though honour's lost
  At murder's cost
 It fills the grave with me."

The story finish'd, the fire low,
Threw out a faint and dying glow;
And both in silence ponder'd long,
Upon the tale of punish'd wrong.
So deep and fast their minds in thought,
That they in sleep were gently caught,
And so the night crept on apace
To greet the morn with freshen'd face.

END.

POEMS.

The Nightingale.

"Twas dawn, and great Sahara lay
   Cool'd 'neath the moon's endearing light ;
As on the desert's sterile way,
   In hopeless humour from his plight,
A trav'ller, lost to human pow'r,
Breath'd out his last earth-number'd hour.

Quick flash'd life's mem'ries thro' his mind,
   Inspiring hope and fell despair ;
Surging they came, and both combin'd,
   Were mingled with his dying pray'r :
As silent and wond'ring the soul,
Linger'd before its final goal.

Surely the awful sleep of death
   Gives to the soul its lasting form ;
Shap'd by its own escaping breath,
   For realms of peace or ceaseless storm :
So his, pass'd to tranquility,
Forbode a heav'nly liberty.

Fair came a vision to his eyes,
   Dimm'd to all-ruling nature there ;
Of home, of friends, and native skies,
   And youth's unconscious ride with care :
Full in its emptiness of state,
The world was there ; its king was Fate.

What brighter vision could we deem
   More soothing to immortal fear
Than boyhood's vain imprison'd dream ?
   The innocence of life's career :
What greater boon could man have given,
Than passage through his home to heaven.

So by the homestead of his birth,
  His spirit wander'd in its flight;
While o'er the rich and fertile earth,
  That desert moon shone fair and bright:
And softly, with a murmur kind,
The night was voic'd with southern wind.

High on the midnight air was heard
  A sweet, though melancholy song;
Transmitted to the skies a bird
  Sang as the spirit swept along:
And to that sad imploring strain,
The heav'ns op'd and shut amain.

Calmly the night declin'd, and morn
  Burst with refreshen'd force around;
And earth, to new endeavours born,
  Was with their execution bound:
But where was he in light of day,
Who tun'd that nightingale's lay?

The Brothers.

Two brothers went sailing the world to find
  What most were their heart's desires;
Their home and their friends were left behind,
      As over the sea,
      Right merrily
  They sought their heart's desires.

In safety they journey'd, but soon were cast
  Adrift on a foreign shore;
And now they thought of the happy past,
      Of many a scene
      That long had been
  Buried in years before.

One brother went seeking for countless wealth,
  For that was his heart's desire ;
He paid no heed to the voice of health,
    Too stubbornly bold,
    That cry for gold,
It was his heart's desire.

The other went seeking for labour strong,
  For that was his heart's desire ;
He lov'd to hear the beautiful song
    Of linnet and thrush,
    In hawthorn bush :
It was his heart's desire.

The first brother, after long years had sped,
  Obtain'd what his heart desir'd ;
But grey, grey hairs, clung around his head,
    He was ag'd and bent,
    In discontent,
Through what his heart desir'd.

The second he took him a lovely wife
  To brighten his heart's desire ;
And liv'd a contented, happy life,
    With little ones there
    To smooth his hair,
And bless his heart's desire.

Through the Moonlit Vespers.

Through the moonlit vesper dreaming
  Of the golden day's decline ;
Was my mind, with beauty seeming,
  Wrapt within a spell divine.
Sooth'd from sorrow's dismal wooing,
  And from all my worldly care ;
Heard I ringdoves gently cooing,
  In yon tree, a loving pair.

And I sought the night above me,
  And upon the heav'ns gaz'd ;
' Is there anyone to love me ? '
  Were the burning words I rais'd ;
And a voice came swiftly flying,
  Though devoid of earthly sound ;
Which in simple words replying,
  ' Love was visible around.'

The Butterfly.
(CRADLE SONG).

DAILY,
  Gayly
    In the sun beams ;
Through the bright meadows and over the streams :
    Creeping
    Sleeping
  On a sweet flow'r,
Taking advantage of ev'ry fine hour.

    Dancing
    Prancing
  When the wind's high ;
Down to the ground, and then up to the sky :
    Thinking
    Winking
  At the old bee,
For working so hard in its liberty.

    Slightly
    Lightly
  What has been done ?
Winter storms blowing and summer winds gone ;
    Snugly
    Ugly
  Not e'er a wing,
Where's the fine butterfly, poor little thing.

The Prince and the Fly,

THE battle's strife no more is heard,
　And silence reigns around ;
The victor's sleep is well assur'd,
　Upon the hard-fought ground.

The beaten flee, a straggling band,
　In order to evade
The death that seeks them thro' the land,
　By the avenging blade.

Their prince a wanderer is he,
　A price is on his head,
His heart is crushed with misery,
　Alas ! his hopes are dead.

Lo ! proud was he a day before,
　With thoughts of victory,
As riding gaily to the war,
　A soldier great and free.

But now he roams the silent glade,
　The forest is his home ;
He sinks beneath their gloomy shade,
　With faintness—overcome.

And while asleep, his foes appear,
　And near his mossy bed ;
He'sleeps so sound, he does not hear
　That heavy martial tread.

Yet there is One above who sees
　; His foemen in the wood,
Wending their way beneath the trees,
　Eager to spill his blood.

His voice speaks from the lofty sky,
   Yet heard by only one ;
He whispers to the little fly,
   His orders——to be done.

The fly obeys, and lights upon
   The sleeping prince's nose ;
Buzz! buzz! hum! hum! the work is done,
   He wakes from his repose.

Up, up he starts, for near him stand,
   Three foemen brave and strong,
Each firmly grasping in his hand,
   A weapon bright and long.

The prince's sword is quickly drawn ;
   'Tis death or liberty ;
And soon upon the ground is strewn,
   The corpses of those three.

He wipes his blade, and with a sigh,
   Ponders upon that strife—
He does not think a little fly,
   Preserved his hunted life.

THORNTON AND PEARSON, THE COLLEGE PRESS, BRADFORD.